KWEP
11/11

W9-BHZ-985

FORTUNE COOKIE FORTUNES

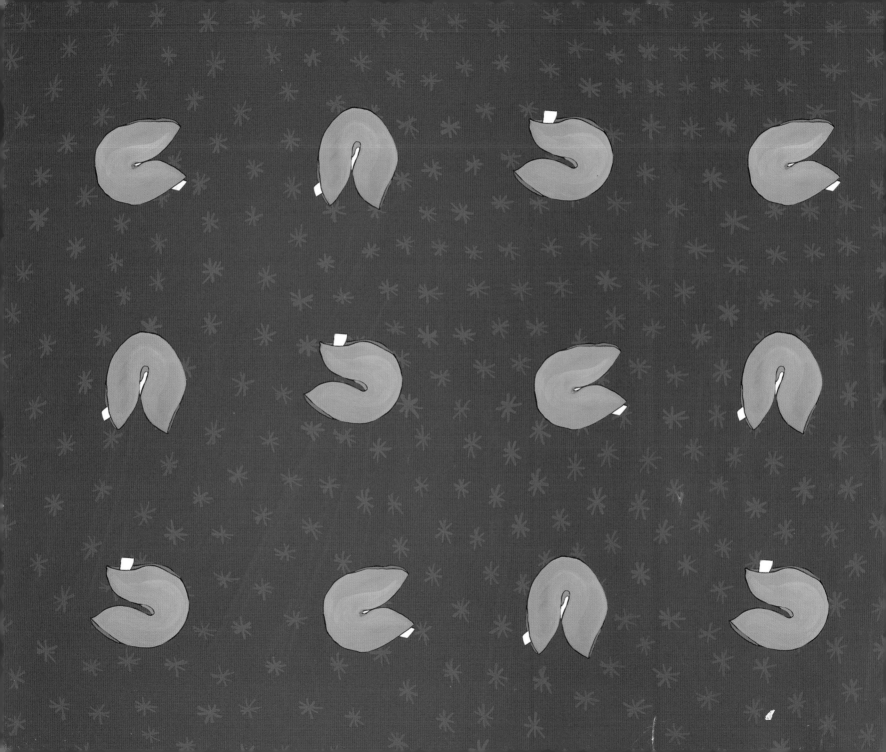

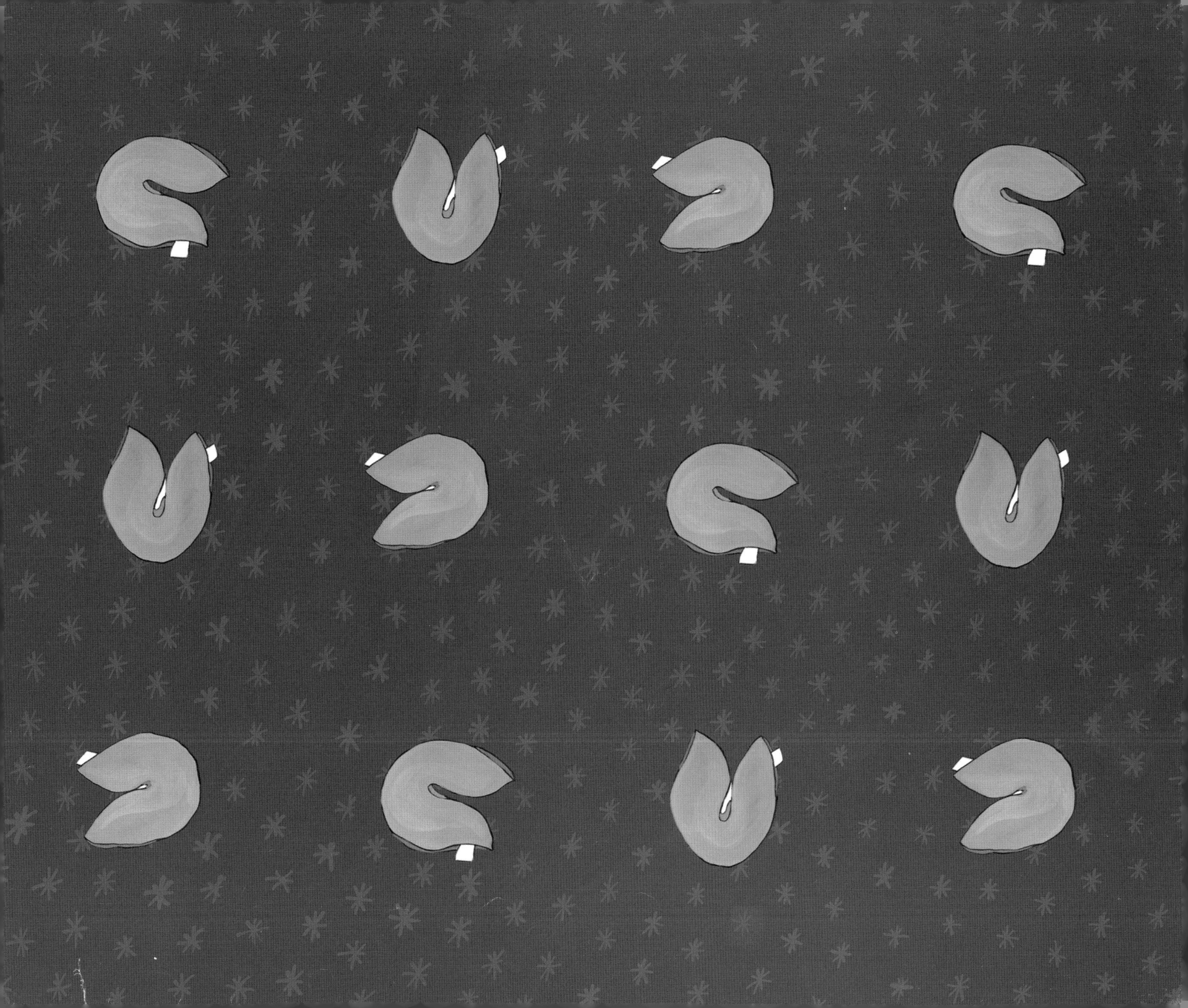

To RISD & Fred Lynch's Fortune Cookie Assignment

Copyright © 2004 by Grace Lin

All rights reserved. Published in the United States by
Dragonfly Books, an imprint of Random House
Children's Books, a division of Random House, Inc.,
New York. Originally published in hardcover in the
United States by Alfred A. Knopf, an imprint of
Random House Children's Books, a division of
Random House, Inc., New York, in 2004

Dragonfly Books with the colophon is a registered
trademark of Random House, Inc.

Visit us on the Web! www.randomhouse.com/kids

Educators and librarians, for a variety of teaching
tools, visit us at www.randomhouse.com/teachers

Library of Congress Cataloging-in-Publication Data
Lin, Grace.
Fortune cookie fortunes / Grace Lin.
p.   cm.
Summary: After a young Chinese American
girl opens fortune cookies with her family,
she notices that the fortunes seem to
come true. Includes brief notes on the
history of the fortune cookie.
ISBN 978-0-375-81521-8 (hardcover)
ISBN 978-0-375-91521-5 (lib. bdg.)
ISBN 978-0-440-42192-4 (pbk.)
[1. Fortune cookies—Fiction.
2. Chinese Americans—Fiction.]
I. Title.
PZ7.L644Fo 2004 [E]—dc21
2003009011

MANUFACTURED IN CHINA

12 11 10 9 8 7 6 5 4

FORTUNE COOKIE FORTUNES

GRACE LIN

DRAGONFLY BOOKS
NEW YORK

The best part about eating at a Chinese restaurant is the fortune cookies.
Crack! Crack! Crack!
What will our fortunes say?

"How do you think your fortune will come true, Ba-Ba?" Mei-Mei asks.

"It won't come true," Jie-Jie scoffs. "They never come true."

But I'm not so sure. . . .

The next day, Ba-Ba and I go to the park. "I'm tired," he says, and suddenly I am too. But before I fall asleep, I remember Ba-Ba's fortune:

☺ Your moods are contagious.

When I get back, I go see Ma-Ma.
"The garden is growing so well,"
Ma-Ma says. "It must be the
new fertilizer I'm using."
But her fortune was . . .

☺ Attention and care will make great things happen.

I peek into Jie-Jie's room.
What is she doing?

☺ Your imagination will create many friends.

Then I watch
Mei-Mei refill the
bird feeder. . . .

☺ Your smallest action will attract many.

Everyone's fortune is coming true!
What about mine? Do I see the world
in a different way?

Depart not from the path that fate has assigned you.

You are on the road to your heart's desire.

Your destiny lies before you; choose wisely.

Will I always see the world this way?
There's only one way to find out. . . .

☺ You like Chinese food.

A pleasant experience is ahead; don't pass it by.

Crack!

Time for another fortune cookie!
What will it say?

☺ Look forward to a life of great fortune!

I think fortune cookie fortunes are always true, don't you?

Fortune cookies

Fortune cookies can be considered one of the first true Asian American foods. Associated with Chinese cuisine and Asian culture, the fortune cookie actually originated in the United States in the early 20th century.

The birth of the fortune cookie has many conflicting legends. Most credit David Jung for creating the treat as a promotional device, in 1918, for his Hong Kong Noodle Company in Los Angeles. Others claim that in 1914 a Japanese inventor, Makoto Hagiwara (who intended it as a refreshment at San Francisco's Japanese Tea Garden), introduced the cookie and that local Chinese restaurants seized upon the idea when forced to think of a dessert for tourists.

Fortune cookies do have roots in Chinese culture. The fortune cookie can be seen as a modern reinvention of the moon cake, a round cake eaten at the Mid-Autumn Festival. In the 13th and 14th centuries in China, secret messages were delivered in moon cakes. During the American railway boom in the late 19th century, Chinese workers exchanged biscuits bearing words of encouragement instead of moon cakes at the Mid-Autumn Festival. And thus, the jump to fortune cookies was inevitable.

However, one can trace the fortune cookie to Japanese culture as well. The Japanese New Year custom of receiving good fortunes in a flat, light cracker called a *sembei* can easily be seen as the inspiration for the fortune cookie. The *sembei* is unsweetened, though. Many claim sugar was added to the fortune cookie to appeal to America's sweet tooth.

Regardless, the fortune cookie has been baked into contemporary Asian American culture. Love, wealth, health, luck—all of life's virtues have found themselves imprinted in one shape or form inside the delectable, memorable fortune cookie!

☺ You have just read a good book.